HEY, PRESTO!

Nadia Shireen

JONATHAN CAPE • LONDON

For
Linus

HEY, PRESTO!

A JONATHAN CAPE BOOK 978 1 780 08002 4

Published in Great Britain by Jonathan Cape,
an imprint of Random House Children's Books
A Random House Group Company
This edition published 2012
1 3 5 7 9 10 8 6 4 2
Copyright © Nadia Shireen, 2012
The right of Nadia Shireen to be identified
as the author of this work has been
asserted in accordance with the Copyright,
Designs and Patents Act 1988.

RANDOM HOUSE CHILDREN'S BOOKS
61–63 Uxbridge Road, London W5 5SA
www.kidsatrandomhouse.co.uk   www.randomhouse.co.uk
Addresses for companies within The Random House Group Limited
can be found at: www.randomhouse.co.uk/offices.htm
THE RANDOM HOUSE GROUP Limited Reg. No. 954009
A CIP catalogue record for this book is available
from the British Library.
Printed in China

Presto and Monty didn't have much, but it didn't matter.
They were best friends and they were happy.

twang twang twang

Monty was good at singing,

eating ice cream

and pulling extremely silly faces,

while Presto had a most unusual talent.
With the help of a battered old hat
and a slightly wonky wand . . .

. . . he was a brilliant MAGICIAN.

One day, Monty saw a poster that made him *very* excited.
"We'll put on a magic show and become famous!"
he hooted. "And we won't be poor or smelly any more."

So they packed up Presto's
battered old hat and
slightly wonky wand,
and set off.

When they got there,
the carnival was quite busy.

"I know!" said Monty, bouncing up
and down. "We should take it in turns
to be the star of the show. I'll go first."

So Monty shouted
in his loudest voice,

ROLL UP, ROLL UP!

hook-a-duck

Presto hid behind
him and made sure
all the magic tricks
worked perfectly.

Presto waited patiently for
his turn to be on stage. But
it never seemed to happen.
It was Monty's turn, night . . .

after night . . .

after
night . . .

The magic show was a great
success. But something odd
had happened to Monty.

He had become bossy,

rude and demanding.

Presto wasn't enjoying himself any more.

Soon, thanks to Presto, Monty was famous.
He was offered a big bag of money to put on
THE BIGGEST MAGIC SHOW EVER.
It would even be on television.

"I'm going to be a super-duper megastar!"
said Monty. "And this time, Presto,
you'll even get to be on stage!"

But Presto didn't want to be sawn
in half – ESPECIALLY by Monty.
He picked up his battered old hat and
his slighty wonky wand, and left the
carnival for good.

The next day, it was **SHOWTIME!**

"Hey, Presto!"
Monty called.
But his friend
had disappeared.

"Humph," said Monty. "Well, I'm the star around here. Who needs him anyway?"

He bought himself a shiny new hat,

found a very fancy magic wand

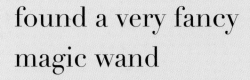

and quickly read a big book about magic tricks.

Back at home, Presto wondered
if Monty didn't need him after all.

But Monty's show didn't
get off to a good start . . .

And it went from bad . . .

. . . to worse.

Presto couldn't bear it
any longer.

"Oh, Presto, I wish you were here!" said Monty. "You'd get me out of this pickle. If only I hadn't been such a big-headed oaf."

But then . . .

HEY PRESTO!

Presto finally made his entrance.

The crowd went wild.

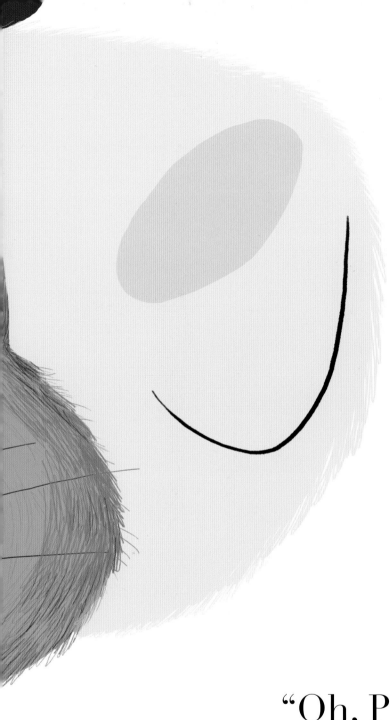

"Oh, Presto!" said Monty.
"I've missed you so much!"

Presto gave a contented purr, and
Monty promised that things would
be different from now on.

And that's how the friends cooked up a brand-new act,

PRESTO &

MAGIC!

OoooOH!

. . . they put on the perfect show.